I0783490

THE LEGEND OF SLEEPY HOLLOW

Revised for Younger Readers by
Michelle Lemke Riggs

Based on the essay written in 1819 by
Washington Irving

Living Popups illustrated and
AUGMENTED REALITY enabled

Living Popups

Augmented reality popups featuring the voices of:

Deirdre Knickerbocker Jessie Gill
Teddy Knickerbocker Theo Hamm
Ichabod Crane Tom Payne
Brom Bones Steven Weber

Produced by Living Popups, Inc.:

Cheryl Bayer   Sara Delgado   Michelle Riggs
Thomas Bergstig   Jamie Dixon   Nigel Rodriguez
Aaron Booker   Isaac Middleton   Erwin Umali
Ken Pellegrino

- Get the app -
Search **LP Bookspace** on iOS and Android

livingpopups.page.link/lpbookspace

Welcome

Welcome to the Living Popups illustrated and augmented reality enabled printing of *The Legend of Sleepy Hollow*, re-Imagined for younger readers by **Michelle Lemke Riggs** and based on the essay written by Washington Irving in 1819.

The story is set in 1790 in the countryside around the Dutch settlement of Tarry Town, New York. Sleepy Hollow is known for its ghosts and the haunting atmosphere that pervades the imaginations of its inhabitants and visitors.

The augmented reality companion features the great-great-great grandchildren of Diedrich Knickerbocker, the original chronicler of this legend.

They provide insights and interesting facts along the way to help the reader with comprehension and to gain a better understanding of the story.

There are also occasional visits from two of the main characters, Ichabod Crane and Brom Bones - not to mention the Headless Horseman!

Simply start the app*, select Sleepy Hollow, point the camera at the illustrations and let the characters from *The Legend of Sleepy Hollow* take it from there!

Search the iOS and Android app-stores for
LP Bookspace

AR Enabled Illustrations

Followed by a *Behind the Scenes* section.

Welcome to
Sleepy
Hollow

The following story was found among the papers
of the late Diedrich Knickerboker…

If you travel north of New York City about 20 miles, you will come upon the Tappan "Zee" (the Dutch word for sea), where the Hudson River widens to about three miles across. Not far from here is a little valley which is one of the quietest places in the whole world. A small brook glides through it, with just enough murmur to lull a person to sleep, and the occasional tapping of a woodpecker is the only sound that breaks the stillness. It's the perfect place to dream.

This drowsy, dreamy glen is known by the
name of Sleepy Hollow, and the people who live
there often see strange sights and hear music and
voices in the air. The whole neighborhood is full of
ghost stories, haunted spots, and superstitions.
Shooting stars and meteors flash across the night
sky more often in this valley than in any other part
of the country. Even visitors--no matter how wide
awake they are before they enter--are sure to

breathe the drowsy Sleepy Hollow air and grow imaginative, dreaming dreams and seeing phantoms. The entire, secluded place has an atmosphere of being under a spell and filled with spirits.

The main spirit that haunts this enchanted region is the ghost of a headless man on horseback. People say he is the ghost of a soldier whose head was carried away by a cannon ball in a Revolutionary War battle. Country folk see him hurrying along on a gloomy night, as if on the wings of the wind. He haunts not only the valley but the nearby roads and especially the church. Some say the body of the soldier was buried in the churchyard, so the ghost rides to the scene of battle every night in search of his head. Then, in a hurry to get back to the churchyard before sunrise, he rushes along the Hollow with great speed, like a midnight blast. This tale of superstition is so legendary that the ghost is known throughout the countryside as the Headless Horseman of Sleepy Hollow.

Sleepy Hollow is one of those small valleys in New York where the old customs and traditions remain the same, unlike the constant changes happening in other parts of the country. It's like a little nook of still water bordering a rapid stream, undisturbed by the rush of the passing current. And to this peaceful spot, one man named Ichabod Crane arrived to teach the children and bring the outside world in.

Schoolmaster Crane looked quite like the animal of his name. He was tall but extremely skinny, with narrow shoulders, long arms and legs, hands that dangled a mile out of his sleeves, and feet that might have served for shovels. His head was small and flat on top, with huge ears, large green, glassy eyes, and a long beak nose. To see him striding along a hill on a windy day, with his clothes fluttering about him, one might have thought he was a scarecrow that escaped from a cornfield.

His schoolhouse was one large room, constructed of logs. It was located at the foot of a woody hill, with a brook running close by and a large birch tree growing at one end. From inside, one could overhear the low murmur of his students' voices like the hum of a beehive, interrupted now and then by the stern voice of the schoolmaster, who was very strict with his students.

After school, the schoolmaster spent time with the older boys, and on holiday afternoons he walked some of the smaller boys home, especially if they had older sisters to consider for marriage or good food to eat for dinner. His school salary was small, and although he was skinny, he was a big eater, like an anaconda stretching to eat its meal.

According to the customs of the time, he lived for
a week each at the homes of his students. In this
way, he made his way around the neighborhood,

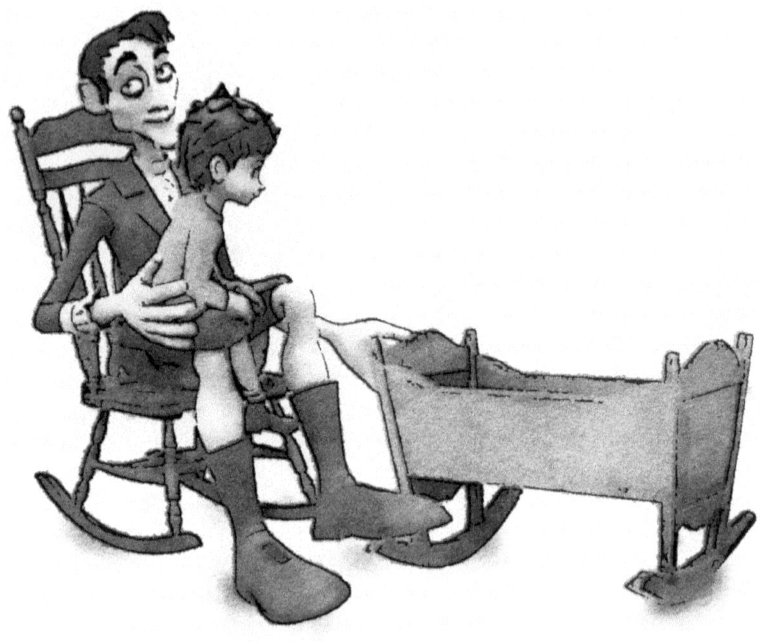

with all of his belongings tied up in a
handkerchief. He shared the local gossip from
household to household. To help repay the families
for their hospitality, he sometimes assisted the
farmers with the easier chores, such as making hay,
mending fences, watering the horses, and cutting
wood for the winter fire. To win over the mothers,
he put aside his stern classroom personality, and
instead he was wonderfully gentle and flattering.
He played with the children, especially the

youngest, and would even hold a child on one knee while rocking a cradle with his other foot for hours.

Ichabod Crane was also the singing-master of the neighborhood and made extra money teaching voice lessons. He was very proud to take his place in front of the church on Sundays with his chosen group of singers. In his own mind, his voice was supreme to all others, and to be sure, his voice sounded loudly above the rest of the congregation. In fact, on Sundays, peculiar quivers can still be heard echoing in that church and even a half mile off across the pond, all said to have echoed from the nose of Ichabod Crane.

All the county girls flocked around him after church on Sunday, making the local boys envious. Ichabod himself was quite happy when surrounded by the smiles of the local ladies and enjoyed the excitement his presence brought about. The women of this rural neighborhood were quite taken with the schoolmaster because he was smart and well-educated--he had read several books all the way to the end!--and therefore appeared more sophisticated than the locals.

In fact, Ichabod Crane was a peculiar mix of childlike and clever. He had an appetite for the supernatural and was spellbound by such stories. Living in Sleepy Hollow only increased his fascination with otherworldly tales. After school, it was often his pleasure to lie in the pasture next to the brook reading ghost stories. He stayed till dusk, when his imagination frightened him as he walked

home through swamp, stream, and woodland. Every sound of nature--the cry of the tree toad, the hooting of the screech owl, the sudden rustling of birds frightened from their roost--made his heart pound with adrenaline and delight. To battle his fright, he loudly sang church tunes in his nasally tone, which the people of Sleepy Hollow were amazed to hear floating from the hilltop to their homes.

Another of his fearful pleasures was to spend long winter evenings with the old wives while they spun tales by the fire. As apples roasted and spluttered in the fire, he listened to their marvelous

tales of ghosts and goblins and haunted fields, brooks, and bridges, and particularly of the Headless Horseman. He would equally delight and frighten them with tales of comets and shooting stars, and with the alarming fact that the world absolutely did spin around--they were upside down half the time!

However, all this tale-telling while safe next to the fire came at a price: the walk home afterwards was terrifying. What fearful shapes and shadows crossed his path in the ghostly glare of a snowy night! How often was he startled by some snow-covered shrub which looked like a ghost! How often did his own steps on the frosty crust make him look with dread over his shoulder, expecting to find some creature following close behind him! And how often was he thrown into despair by some rushing blast of wind howling among the trees, convincing him that the Headless Horseman was on one of his nightly rides!

These were all terrors of the night, though, and daylight ended those nightmares. He would have had a pleasant life, in fact, had he not crossed paths with someone that caused him more confusion than all the ghosts and ghouls combined: Katrina Van Tassel.

Katrina was one of his music pupils, the daughter and only child of a wealthy farmer named

Baltus Van Tassel. She was beautiful in every way, and famous not only for her beauty, but also for her family's fortune.

Ichabod Crane had a soft heart, and he soon favored Katrina, especially after he visited her at her father's mansion. Baltus Van Tassel was a successful and content farmer, thinking little about the world outside his farm. He kept his own home snug, happy, and well-kept. He was satisfied with his wealth but not proud about it, and he was happy with the abundance he provided for his family.

The Van Tassel home was located on the banks of the Hudson River, in a green, sheltered nook. A great elm tree spread its broad branches over it, and at its foot bubbled up a spring of the sweetest water, which sparkled through the grass to a nearby brook. Near the farmhouse was a large barn that could have served as a church thanks to its size. Every corner of it seemed to be bursting with the treasures of the farm. Troops of pigs grunted in their pens; a squadron of snowy geese floated in an adjoining pond along with whole fleets of ducks; regiments of turkeys gobbled through the farmyard, and guinea fowl pecked about. In front of the barn door strutted the rooster, a warrior clapping his wings and crowing with the pride and gladness of his heart.

Ichabod's mouth watered as he looked upon this splendid promise of delicious winter meals. In his devouring mind's eye, he pictured every pig roasted on a platter with an apple in its mouth, the

geese swimming in their own gravy, and the ducks laid out on dishes and drizzled with sauce. He imagined future sides of bacon, a juicy ham, a trussed up turkey, savory sausages, and even the rooster himself sprawled in a dish. In addition to these riches, he rolled his green eyes over the meadow lands: the rich fields of wheat, rye, buckwheat, and corn, and the orchards heavy with fruit.

When Ichabod entered the house, his desire to be master of the home was complete. It was a spacious farmhouse, with a large front porch fully equipped for animal caretaking and fishing. It held a butter churn, a spinning wheel, and long benches for lounging in the summer. Inside the home were more riches: a huge bag of wool ready to be spun, ears of corn, and strings of dried apples, peaches, and red peppers. An open door to the parlor gave him a peek at claw-footed chairs and dark mahogany tables that shone like mirrors, along with a corner cupboard left open to display treasures of antique silver and china.

His heart yearned for the young woman who would inherit these wonders, and his imagination went wild with the idea of selling everything and investing the money in vast acres of land in the wilderness. He imagined a whole family of children, mounted on top of a wagon loaded with household goods, pots and kettles dangling beneath it, and himself riding a majestic mare, setting out for Kentucky, Tennessee, or who knows where!

Ichabod's only obstacle to these riches was gaining the affections of the daughter of Van Tassel, the fair Katrina. However, he had more difficulties ahead than a knight in shining armor from the past, who only had to conquer giants, wizards, and fiery dragons before making his way through iron gates and castle walls to reach the lady of his heart, who then of course married him. Instead, Ichabod had to win his way to the heart of a popular and wealthy country lady! In addition, he had to face a group of other admirers who kept a watchful and angry eye on each other as they competed for her affections.

Among Katrina's admirers was a burly, roaring, swaggering man by the name of Abraham Van Brunt, otherwise known as Brom, the hero of the countryside, well known for his feats of strength and toughness. He was broad-shouldered, with short curly black hair and a face that held a look of both fun and arrogance. For his looks and muscle, he had been given the nickname Brom Bones. He was famous for his great knowledge and skill in horsemanship and for winning at all contests and races. As the strongest man in the countryside, he was the umpire in all disputes, giving his decisions with a tone that allowed no argument. He was

always ready for either a fight or a frolic, but with
all his roughness, he was also full of good humor.
He was made more of mischief than of ill will.

Brom Bones had three best friends who looked
to him as their role model, and the group of them
were present at every fight and every party for
miles around. Sometimes he and his crew could be
heard dashing along past the farmhouses at
midnight with whoops and hollers. The
townspeople, startled from their sleep, would listen

for a moment and then exclaim, "Ay, there goes Brom Bones and his gang!" The neighbors looked at him with a mixture of awe and admiration, and when any prank or brawl occurred in the area, they always shook their heads and supposed Brom Bones was at the bottom of it.

Brom had admired Katrina for some time, and it was said that she returned his affection. This was the man with whom Ichabod Crane had to compete. A stronger man would have shrunk from the competition, and a wiser man would have despaired. Ichabod, however, had a happy mix of flexibility and perseverance in his nature. Like the willow, he bent but did not break. Though he bowed to the slightest pressure, once it was removed, he popped back up with his head held high as ever.

He wasn't foolish enough to openly rival Brom Bones, but instead Ichabod was sneakier in his advances. He used his position as voice teacher to make frequent visits to the farmhouse. Baltus Van Tassel loved his daughter and was an indulgent father; he let her have her way in everything. His wife was busy tending house and caring for the poultry, for as she always said, ducks and geese were foolish things and must be looked after, but girls can take care of themselves. So, while her mother bustled about at one end of the house, and Baltus sat at the other end, Ichabod courted their daughter, taking her for a stroll by the side of the spring at twilight.

From the moment Ichabod Crane made his advances, Brom's interest in Katrina seemed to fade. His horse was no longer seen outside the Van Tassel home. However, a deadly feud gradually arose between him and the teacher. Brom would have preferred to settle the matter by a single fight, but Ichabod was too aware of Brom's superior strength to give him the opportunity. He had overheard Brom boasting that he would "double

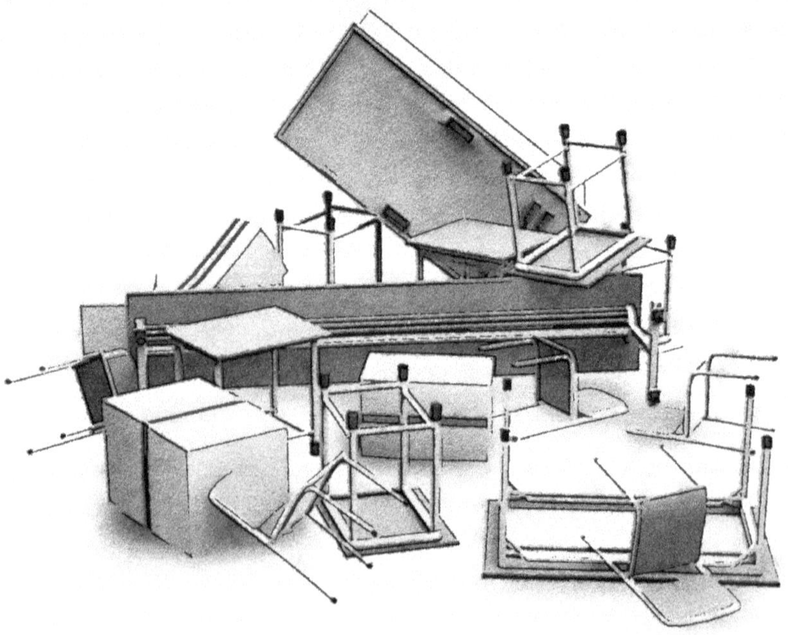

the schoolmaster up and lay him on a shelf of his own schoolhouse," so he made sure there was no chance for a fight. This left Brom with no choice but to use his habits of practical jokes, making Ichabod the object of his gang's attention. They clogged up the chimney of his singing school, so it filled with smoke. They broke into his classroom and turned everything topsy-turvy, and they took every opportunity to make Ichabod look foolish in front of Katrina. Brom even taught a stray dog to whine and howl in a ridiculous way and introduced it as a rival of Ichabod's voice instruction.

Things went on this way for some time, until one beautiful autumn afternoon at school. Ichabod watched over his pupils, his desk covered in confiscated toys, snacks, and tidbits that children used to entertain themselves. The students all worked quietly until a messenger arrived with an invitation for Ichabod to attend a party being held that evening at the Van Tassels' home. Ichabod was so excited that he hurried the students through their lessons. Books were flung aside without being put away on the shelves, inkstands were overturned, benches were thrown down, and he dismissed the whole school an hour early.

Ichabod spent at least an extra half hour grooming himself, brushing off his best (and only) black suit, arranging his hair just so. He even borrowed a horse from the farmer with whom he was currently living, Hans Van Ripper, in order to make a grand appearance like a knight on his steed. In truth, the animal was a broken-down plow-horse that had outlived almost everything but its viciousness. He was skinny and shaggy with a head like a hammer; his rusty mane and tail were tangled and knotted with burs. One eye had lost its pupil and was glaring and ghostly, but the other had the gleam of a genuine devil in it. Named

Gunpowder, he had been a favorite horse of his master's, who was a furious rider and had given some of that spirit to his horse. As old and broken-down as he looked, there was more of a devil lurking in him than in any young filly in the countryside.

Ichabod was a suitable rider for such a steed. He rode with short stirrups, which brought his knees nearly up to the pommel of the saddle; his sharp elbows stuck out like a grasshopper's; he carried his whip like a staff, and as his horse jogged, the motion of his arms was like the flapping of wings. A small wool cap rested on the top of his nose, and the tails of his black coat fluttered behind him almost to the horse's tail. He made quite the picture; such a sight is rarely seen in broad daylight.

It was evening when Ichabod arrived at the Van Tassel mansion, which he found decorated with all the flowery beauty of the countryside. Old farmers with leathery faces wore homemade coats and breeches, blue stockings, and huge shoes with magnificent pewter buckles. Their wives wore caps, long gowns, and homemade petticoats with scissors, pincushions, and pockets hanging on the outside. Their daughters wore similar clothes, with the addition of a straw hat, a fine ribbon, or perhaps a white frock. The sons wore squared-off coats with rows of brass buttons, and their hair was styled in the fashion of the times.

Brom Bones, however, was the hero of the scene, having arrived on his favorite steed, Daredevil. The horse was a creature like Brom who was full of spirit and mischief, and which no one but himself could manage. Brom was noted, in fact, for preferring vicious, tricky animals which kept the rider in constant risk of his neck, and he believed that a well-behaved horse was unworthy of a spirited man.

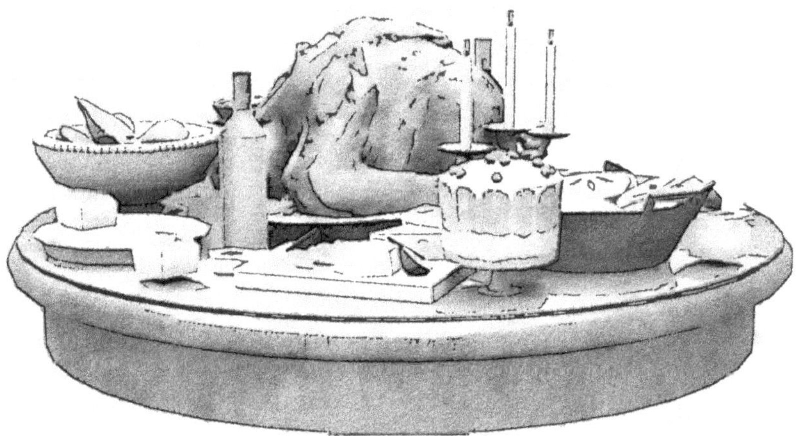

Now, when Ichabod arrived, he was captivated not by the beauty of the landscape nor of the ladies, but by that of the country tea table, filled to overflowing with delectable treats. Such heaped up platters of indescribable cakes! There was the doughty doughnut, the tender olykoek, the crisp and crumbling cruller, sweet cakes and short cakes, ginger cakes and honey cakes...the whole family of cakes! And then there were apple pies, peach pies, and pumpkin pies, slices of ham and smoked beef, and delicious dishes of preserved plums and peaches and pears and quinces, not to mention broiled fish and roasted chickens, with bowls of milk and cream, and a teapot sending up clouds of vapor from the midst of it all.

Happily, Ichabod tasted every dish. He was a kind and thankful creature, whose heart grew in proportion as he filled with good cheer and good food. He couldn't help rolling his large eyes round as he ate and chuckling with the possibility that he might one day be lord of all this almost unimaginable luxury and splendor. Then, he thought, how soon he'd quit the old schoolhouse, and he wouldn't even invite the new schoolmaster to his parties!

Old Baltus Van Tassel moved about among his guests feeling content and in a good mood, round and jolly as the harvest moon. His attentions to each guest were brief: a handshake, a slap on the shoulder, a loud laugh, and an invitation to help themselves. The sound of the music from the common room called for partygoers to dance. The musician, who had been the single-handed orchestra of the neighborhood for more than half a century, had an instrument that was as old and battered as himself. The majority of the time, he scraped on two or three strings, moving his head with every movement of the bow and stamping his foot whenever a fresh couple started dancing.

Ichabod prided himself on his dancing as much as on his vocal powers. Not a limb about him was still, and to have seen his wiry frame in full motion

clattering about the room, one would have thought that the patron saint of dance was appearing in person. The lady of his heart was his dance partner and smiling graciously at him, while Brom Bones, full of love and jealousy, sat brooding by himself in a corner.

When the dance ended, Ichabod was drawn to a group of older folks, including Old Van Tassel, who were reminiscing about the past and telling long stories about the war. The British and American line had run near the neighborhood, and just enough time had passed since the war to allow each storyteller to dress up his tale with a little fiction and make himself the hero of his story.

But all these were nothing compared to the ghost stories that followed. The neighborhood was rich in legends. The nearness of Sleepy Hollow no doubt contributed to the number of supernatural stories. It was like there was a contagion in the air that blew from that haunted region. Several people from Sleepy Hollow were present at Van Tassel's and, as usual, were telling their wild and wonderful legends. Many tales were told about wailings heard and wisps seen around the great tree where the unfortunate Major Andre was taken prisoner during the Revolutionary War. The neighborhood people regarded the tree, which was now known as Major Andre's Tree, with a mixture of respect and superstition, partly out of sympathy for Major Andre, and partly from the tales of strange sights connected to it. Some mention was also made of the Woman in White, who haunted the dark glen at Raven Rock and was often heard shrieking on winter nights before a storm, having died there in the snow herself. However, the stories mainly revolved around the favorite ghost of Sleepy Hollow, the Headless Horseman.

He had been heard several times recently, patrolling the countryside and tying his horse nightly among the graves in the churchyard. The isolated location of this church made it a favorite haunt of troubled ghosts. The church stood on a hill, surrounded by trees. On one side of the church ran a large brook among broken rocks and fallen tree trunks. Over a deep black part of the stream, not far from the church, was a wooden bridge. The road that led to the bridge was thickly shaded by overhanging trees, which cast a gloom over it even in the daytime and brought a fearful darkness to it by night.

As one of the favorite haunts of the Headless Horseman, this area was the place where he was

seen the most often. The tale was told of old
Brower, who didn't believe in ghosts, and how he
met the Horseman returning from his trip into
Sleepy Hollow. They galloped over hill and swamp
until they reached the bridge. Then, the Horseman
suddenly turned into a skeleton, threw old Brower
into the brook, and sprang away over the treetops
with a clap of thunder!

Brom Bones had a story of his own, and of course he wasn't afraid of the Headless Horseman. He claimed that while returning one night from a

nearby village, he was overtaken by this midnight trooper. Brom offered to race him, and he would have won, too, as Daredevil was beating the goblin horse all through the Hollow, but just as they came to the church bridge, the Horseman bolted and vanished in a flash of fire.

All these tales were told in low voices in the dark, with the faces of the listeners flashing in the firelight. The stories sank deep in Ichabod's mind. He even told stories of his own about the fearful sights which he had seen himself during his nightly walks around Sleepy Hollow.

The party eventually broke up, and the old farmers gathered their families in their wagons and rattled home over the distant hills. The laughter of young people mingled with the clatter of hoofs, sounding fainter and fainter until the party scene was silent. Ichabod stayed behind to have a private chat with the heiress Katrina, convinced he was on the path to marriage.

No one knows for sure what was said during this meeting. However, one can guess the beautiful Katrina turned down his proposal. Shortly afterward, Ichabod left the mansion looking sad and disappointed. Without looking around to notice the scene of wealth that he loved, he went straight to the stable. With several hearty kicks, he rudely woke his borrowed steed from its peaceful sleep.

It was the witching hour when heavy-hearted Ichabod began his travels home along the same path he had traveled so happily that very afternoon. The night was as dreary as he was. Far below him, the Tappan Zee spread its dark waters. In the dead hush of midnight, he could faintly hear the barking of a dog on the other side of the Hudson. No signs of life occurred near him except the occasional chirp of a cricket or twang of a bullfrog.

All the stories of ghosts and goblins that he had heard in the afternoon now came crowding into his mind. The night grew darker and darker. The stars seemed to sink deeper in the sky, and heavy clouds occasionally hid them altogether. Ichabod had never felt so lonely and gloomy. He was now approaching the very spot where many of the ghost stories had taken place.

In the center of the road stood an enormous tree, Major Andre's tree, which towered like a giant above all the other trees of the neighborhood. Its limbs were gnarled and fantastic, large enough to form trunks for ordinary trees, twisting down almost to the earth and rising again into the air.

As Ichabod approached this fearful tree, he began to whistle. He thought he heard someone whistle back! But no, it was only a blast of wind

sweeping through the dry branches. Then, he saw something white hanging in the tree! He paused to look but found that it was a place where the tree had been scarred by lightning. He heard a groan, and his teeth chattered, and his knees clutched the saddle! But it was only the rubbing of one huge tree branch upon another in the breeze. He passed the tree safely, but now new dangers lay before him.

About two hundred yards from the tree, a small brook crossed the road and ran into a marshy and thickly-wooded glen called Wiley's Swamp. A few rough logs laid side by side as a bridge over this stream. On the side of the road where the brook entered the woods, a group of oaks and chestnut trees, covered with wild grape vines, created a cavern over it. Passing this bridge was the most frightening test because this is where the captors hid when they surprised and took Major Andre. Ever since, it has been considered a haunted stream, and all those who have to pass it alone after dark are fearful of the place.

As he approached the stream, Ichabod's heart began to thump. He summoned up all his courage, gave his horse a few swift kicks, and attempted to dash quickly across the bridge. However, instead of moving forward, the old mare moved sideways and ran along the fence! Ichabod, whose fears were increasing with each moment, jerked the reins and kicked his foot, but the horse only plunged to the opposite side of the road into a thicket of brambles! The schoolmaster now used both whip and heel on the poor ribs of old Gunpowder, who dashed forward, then came to an abrupt halt just by the bridge and nearly threw Ichabod over his head! Just at this moment, a sound caught Ichabod's ear. In the dark shadow of the grove, on the edge of the brook, he saw something huge, misshapen, and towering. It didn't

move, but it seemed to be gathered up in the gloom, like some gigantic monster ready to spring upon the traveler.

The hair rose on Ichabod's head. What could he do? It was too late to turn and speed away.

Besides, what chance was there of escaping a goblin that could ride on the wind?

He gathered his wits and demanded, "Who are you?" but received no reply.

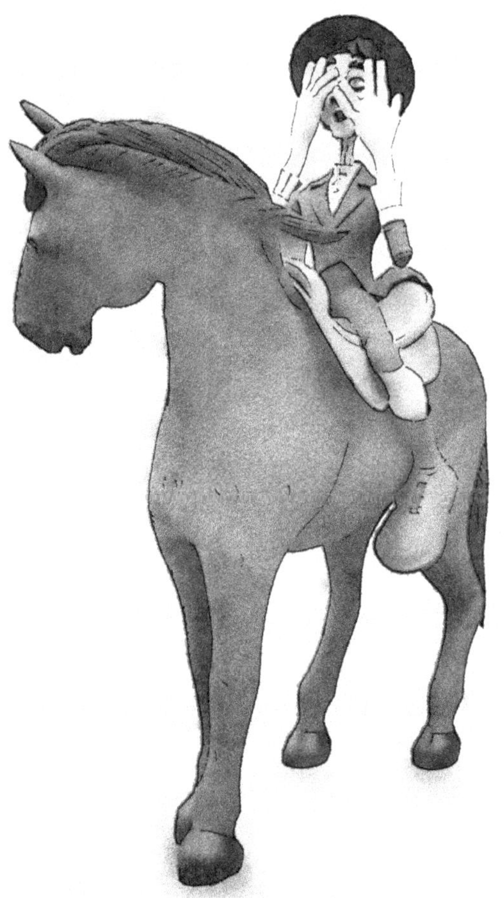

He repeated his demand in a more agitated voice.

Still there was no answer.

Once more he kicked at the immoveable Gunpowder, shut his eyes, and broke out enthusiastically in song.

Just then, the shadowy ghost put itself in motion and stood in the middle of the road. Though the night was dark and dismal, the shape of the specter could be determined. He was a large horseman, mounted on a black horse of powerful frame. He made no attempt to attack or speak. He kept to one side of the road alongside old Gunpowder, who was now finally moving forward.

Ichabod, who did not care for this strange midnight companion, now hurried his horse in hopes of leaving him behind. However, the stranger quickened his horse to the same pace. Ichabod pulled up and slowed into a walk, thinking he would lag behind. The stranger did the same. Ichabod's heart sank, and he prepared to sing again, but his dry tongue stuck to the roof of his mouth, so he could not sing a note.

There was something in the silence of this stranger that was mysterious and awful. When they reached higher ground, the stranger's figure stood out against the sky: gigantic in height, muffled in a cloak, and headless! Ichabod's horror was even

greater when he saw that the stranger carried the head on his saddle! Ichabod's terror rose to desperation; he rained a shower of kicks and blows upon Gunpowder, hoping by sudden movement to give his companion the slip, but the goblin took off with him. Away they dashed through the trees, stones flying and sparks flashing at every hoofbeat. Ichabod's coat fluttered in the air as he stretched his long, lanky body over his horse's head in an effort to make him go faster.

They reached the road which turned off to the right to Sleepy Hollow, but Gunpowder, who now seemed possessed himself, turned away from the road and plunged downhill to the left! This road led through a shady, sandy hollow for about a quarter of a mile. There, the road crossed the famous bridge from the neighborhood ghost stories, and just beyond it stood the whitewashed church.

So far old Gunpowder's panic had given his unskilled rider an advantage in the chase, but just as he got halfway through the hollow, the saddle began to slip under Ichabod. He grabbed the pommel, hoping to hold it in place, but he just barely had time to save himself by clutching Gunpowder around the neck before the saddle fell to the ground. He heard it trampled underfoot by his pursuer. For a moment he thought of Hans Van Ripper's anger at losing it, but this was no time for such fears. The goblin was close on his heels, and he had enough to do to stay on the horse. He

slipped to one side and then the other, and
sometimes jolted on the ridge of his horse's
backbone with a force he feared would split him in
half.

An opening in the trees gave him hope that the church was close. He saw the walls of the church dimly glaring under the trees beyond. He recollected the place where Brom Bones's ghostly competitor had disappeared. If I can reach that bridge, I am safe, he thought to himself. Just then, he heard the black steed panting and blowing close behind him; he even believed that he felt its hot breath! Another kick in the ribs, and old Gunpowder sprang upon the bridge, thundered over the planks, and reached the other side. Ichabod looked behind to see if his pursuer would vanish, according to legend, in a flash of fire and brimstone. Instead, he saw the goblin stand in his stirrups and throw his head! Ichabod tried to dodge the terrible missile, but it was too late. It hit his head with a tremendous crash. He tumbled head first into the dust, and Gunpowder, the black steed, and the goblin rider passed by like a whirlwind.

The next morning, the old horse was found without his saddle, his bridle under his feet, calmly eating grass at his master's gate. Ichabod did not make an appearance at breakfast. Dinner came and went, but no Ichabod. Students gathered at the schoolhouse, but no schoolmaster. Hans Van Ripper was beginning to feel uneasy about the fate of his saddle, as well as that of Ichabod, of course. A search party went out on foot and eventually came upon traces of the schoolmaster. On the road leading to the church, they found the saddle trampled in the dirt, the tracks of a horse's hoofs

deeply dented in the road. They traced the tracks to the bridge, and on the bank of the brook they found the unfortunate Ichabod's hat, and close beside it, a shattered pumpkin.

The brook was searched, but the body of the schoolmaster was not discovered. Hans Van Ripper acted as executor of Ichabod's estate and found among his worldly possessions two and a half shirts, two neckties, a couple pairs of stockings, a rusty razor, a book of church songs with many marked pages, and a broken pitch pipe. Whatever money he possessed must have been with him at

the time of his disappearance. As to the books and furniture of the schoolhouse, they belonged to the community, except for the books about magic, dreams, and fortune-telling, in which were found scribbled bits of poems dedicated to Katrina Van Tassel. Hans Van Ripper burned all these in a fire and declared he would never send his children to school again, as obviously no good came of reading and writing.

The mysterious event caused many rumors to fly at the church on Sunday. Knots of gossipers collected in the churchyard, at the bridge, and at the spot where the hat and pumpkin had been found. The stories of others were called to mind, and when compared to this case, the conclusion was made that Ichabod had been carried off by the Headless Horseman. Since he had no family and was not in debt to anyone, no one troubled themselves any more about him. The school was moved to a different location in the hollow, and another teacher took Ichabod's place.

It is true, however, that an old farmer who visited New York a few years later brought home news that Ichabod Crane was still alive. According to the farmer, Ichabod left the neighborhood partly through fear of the goblin and fear of Hans Van Ripper (whose saddle he'd lost), and partly in embarrassment at having been dismissed by the heiress Katrina.

Brom Bones, who married the fair Katrina shortly after Ichabod's disappearance, looked rather satisfied whenever the story of Ichabod was told, and he always burst into a hearty laugh at the

mention of the pumpkin. This led some to suspect he knew more about the matter than he chose to tell.

The old country wives, however, who are the best judges of these matters, maintain to this day that Ichabod was stolen away by the Headless Horseman. It is a favorite story told by the fire in winter. The bridge became an even greater object of superstition, and the road to the church was moved to avoid it. The deserted schoolhouse fell into disrepair and was reported to be haunted by the ghost of the unfortunate teacher. Schoolchildren walking home on a summer evening often imagined hearing his voice at a distance, singing a church melody in the quiet air of Sleepy Hollow.

THE END

POSTSCRIPT

I heard this story at a business meeting in old Manhattan, at which many of the town leaders were present. I attempted to record it in the precise words in which it was told by a pleasant, shabby,

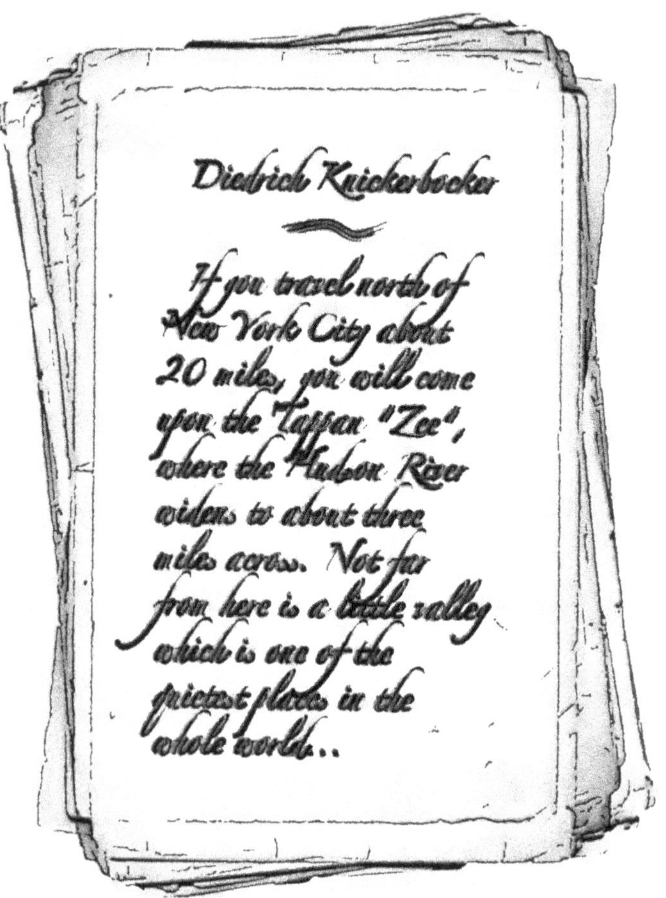

gentlemanly old fellow. He wore tweed clothes and had a sadly humorous face. I strongly suspected he was not used to being in the company of high society because he made such efforts to be entertaining. When his story ended, there was much laughter and praise, especially by those gentlemen who slept through most of the story. However, one tall, dry-looking old gentleman--the sort who never laughs at anything unless with very good reason--remained serious. He leaned forward and asked, "Now, what is the moral of this story? What is its point?"

The storyteller replied, "Why, the point is that there is no situation in life that doesn't have some advantage or pleasure, as long as we're willing to see it, and if you race goblins you will have a rough time of it, and for a country schoolmaster to be refused the hand of an estate heiress is a just outcome."

The old gentleman knit his brows together tightly as he thought over this nonsensical response, while, I thought, the storyteller eyed him with something of a triumphant leer. The gentleman finally replied, "That's all very well, but the story still seems a bit excessive to me, and there are one or two things I doubt can be true."

"Faith, sir," replied the storyteller, "as to that matter, I don't believe one-half of the story myself."

-- D. K.

Living Popups

A look at creating the
AUGMENTED REALITY
characters from:

Behind the Scenes

At Living Popups, we love animating the characters you find in our books.

We start with a script, written by educators who are experts on the subject we're covering and we spend a lot of time refining what the characters say and what they will talk to you about as you read the book.

As we're writing that script, we figure out who the characters will be. We don't only have characters who are in the story! Sometimes we add others that can talk about things from an outside perspective - like a teacher might!

Then we design our characters - the old fashioned way - by drawing them!

Here are the character sketches from Sleepy Hollow.

Once the characters are designed - we model their basic shapes in a 3D program so they can exist inside our AR app.

We add details to the basic shapes…

Then we add color (but printed here in black
and white!)…

That leaves recording actors for the character voices, creating the animation, music and sound design and finally putting it all into the **LP Bookspace** app.

Thank you for enjoying *The Legend of Sleepy Hollow* in augmented reality!

Look for more titles at:

livingpopups.com

*"I'll wait until
it comes out in AR!"*